SCOOTER'S HEART
SWEET, HISTORICAL ROMANCE

PINEVALE VALLEY
BOOK TWO

SARA J WALKER

Scooter's Heart

Copyright © 2024 Sara J. Walker

Edited by: Emily Harmston

Cover by: Glowing Moon Designs

All rights reserved. No part of this story may be reproduced in any form or by any means without the author's prior written consent, except for brief quotations used in reviews.

This is a work of fiction. Names, characters, places, and incidents either are the product of the author's imagination or are used fictitiously. Any resemblance to actual persons, living or dead, events or locales is entirely coincidental.

To the extent that the image or images on the cover of this book depict a person or persons, such person or persons are merely models. They are not intended to portray any character or characters featured in the book.

ABOUT SCOOTER'S HEART

It's November 1928 in the small town of Bakersbee, Georgia. Fifteen-year-old Scooter Wagner longs to escape the mines for a life in medicine, while Mary Maldon, the mine owner's daughter, harbors ambitions of becoming a nurse and helping others.

When tragedy strikes deep in the mine, Scooter and Mary embark on a 260-mile journey to seek aid from a woman skilled in herbal medicine. Their journey ignites a spark between them despite their youth and social differences. But love comes at a price. Mary's father issues an ultimatum that forces Scooter to choose between love and saving his family.

The pair find themselves on separate paths—or so it seems. In a world where coal dust and class barriers threaten to smother hope, can their bond prove strong enough to forge a new future?

CHAPTER ONE

The Appalachian Mountains, 1925

Bakersbee, Georgia

Cool November air prompted Scooter Wagner to button up his wool shirt. It used to be his Sunday shirt, but too many washings of the homespun material had the collar fraying at the edges. Georgia mountain temperatures fluctuated this time of year, but there had been no snow yet, for which he was grateful.

On Saturdays, he hung around the general store hoping to pick up odd jobs, and today, he'd been lucky. The mercantile had a big lumber delivery, and

Mr. Johnson hired him to stay all day and load the wagons for his customers. Hard work but worth the fifty cents plus a few coins from the farmers.

"That's the last, Mr. Smith," Scooter said, settling a pair of planks in Mr. Smith's wagon bed. "If you need help to build the addition, you know where to find me. I'm pretty handy with a hammer."

"I'll keep that in mind, young scamp. Thanks for the help." Mr. Smith tossed him a nickel.

"Thank you, sir," Scooter said, pocketing the coin with a big grin. With that nickel, he was up to seventy-eight cents. Not as much as a miner made in a day, but still pretty good.

The pair of draft horses snorted, and Mr. Smith's wagon rumbled away on the dirt street. Scooter glanced around the bustling streets. The residents of Bakersbee had pitched in the previous summer to build boardwalks between the buildings to keep everyone out of the mud on rainy days. Bakersbee wasn't big, but it was a nice town.

Then he heard a rumble above the normal noises—the rumble of a vehicle. He only knew one person who owned a car. Mr. Reginald Malden, the owner of the general store, Bakersbee mine, and several other mines deep in the hills. And he only came to Bakersbee three or four times a year.

Scooter moved to the front edge of the mercantile's porch to get a good look at the car. He loved cars. His teacher at school found a book for him, and he now knew Mr. Malden's car was a 1924 Packard 8, a real beauty with dark gray paint and wheels with red rims. One day, he wanted to own something like that. Or perhaps a Ford Model T. Scooter wished for a chance to ride in it. Just once.

The vehicle pulled right up to the horse hitch in front of the mercantile, and the sleek, or rather dusty, door swung open. There was no way to keep even the nicest auto clean on these mountain roads.

However, he forgot about the automobile when a young woman stepped out in a layered green dress, matching coat, and fancy buckled low heels. Her shiny brown hair was styled in a smart bob, neatly tucked under a green, bell-shaped cloche hat with a white cloth ribbon tied in an elaborate bow on one side.

The beautiful girl looked to be close to his age of fifteen. Then she glanced his way and caught him staring. She gave him a ghost of a smile, and he barely dipped his chin in response. She was a dream too fine for the likes of him, with his dirty nails and homespun clothes.

"Mary, go get what you need." An annoyed-looking Mr. Malden emerged from the vehicle's front seat. "The drive took longer than expected, and I want to meet with my foreman at five sharp."

Mary Malden.

He hadn't recognized her. But then she'd changed a lot in the last year. He moved closer to the steps leading up to the store entrance and watched as the pair disappeared inside the mercantile.

"Scooter." His mother's voice was sharp behind him.

He spun to see her walking up with her big egg basket, his six-year-old sister beside her. "Has something happened?"

"It's Hetty. That burn she got boiling the soap yesterday is hurting her something fierce. I'm gonna trade some eggs for flour to make her a poultice."

"Scooter," Hetty whined pitifully. Her tear-streaked cheeks broke his heart.

"I'll keep her with me while you go inside," he said.

Ma gave a grateful nod and hurried through the entrance.

Scooter cringed a little at the sight of the tender skin on the girl's forearm. Why hadn't his mother wrapped it? He sat by the rail and patted the wood beside him. "Let's sit on the steps and count the people. Where's your coat?"

"It hurts too much to wear it," she whimpered.

Scooter nodded. "I had a burn once, and it hurt awful. Another day or two, and you'll be right as rain."

"It's like fire." Annie leaned her head on his shoulder and took long, shuddering breaths, her injured arm cradled in her lap.

Before Scooter offered another consolation, the scent of roses washed over him, and he twisted his head in surprise to find Mary Malden crouched on the other side of Hetty.

"Hi, Scooter. Do you remember me? I'm Mary Malden."

"Of ... of course. Yes, ma'am."

She scowled. "Don't ma'am me. We played together as children, and we are both fifteen. Who's this young lady?"

"This is my sister, Hetty."

Mary's brows shot up, and her eyes went wide.

"Ma took in her and her brother, Luke, when I was ten." There was almost no resemblance between Hetty and anyone in their family except her brother. The two of them had alabaster skin covered in freckles and curly red hair, so bright that it was just about orange.

No doubt sensing a sympathetic listener, Hetty's bottom lip trembled. "I got burned."

"Oh, honey, I'm so sorry. I might have something to help."

"You do?" Scooter asked.

Mary sat on the step beside Hetty, and the rose smell washed over him as she dug around in her small reticule. "Here it is." She held up a silver compact triumphantly. "There's a wise woman in Pinevale Valley who grows every type of herb you can imagine. She finds what she can't grow in the forest." She leaned close and whispered, "I like to help her, but Papa doesn't know that."

"What's a wise woman?" Scooter asked.

"Where's Pinevale?" Hetty asked at almost the same time.

Mary's laugh tinkled like a clean brook on a summer day. "Pinevale Valley is where I live. And don't worry, Scooter, Mrs. Kisselton is a God-fearing Christian woman. She knows about plants and how they can help. Sort of a natural physician. Here." She held up the open compact. "It smells nice, and she gave it to me when I burned my fingers on the stove a few days ago. Let's try it on your sister."

Cringing, Hetty bravely stuck out her arm for Mary to dab on some cream.

"It feels better!" The little girl beamed. "Thank you."

"Here, let your brother keep this for you and put it on several times a day until it's better. I'd offer to get you more, but I'm uncertain when we'll return to Bakersbee. Papa was mad when we had a flat tire today. The drive takes ten hours without stops, and we spent the night in Ashville at my aunt's house last night."

"Ten hours?"

"It's two hundred sixty miles from here to Pinevale Valley. Papa let me hold the map. We can't come at all if it snows. The Packard wouldn't make it."

Scooter whistled through his teeth. "Bet that takes a lot of gas."

Mary shrugged. "Papa said it costs almost six dollars one way, what with gas going up to thirty cents a gallon. It's good that his new car gets fifteen miles a gallon."

CLANG-CLANG-CLANG-CLANG

"What's happening?" Mary asked.

"That's the alarm for an emergency at the mine. Will you keep Hetty with you while I help?"

"Of course."

CHAPTER TWO

The ringing of the cast iron bell echoed against the mountaintops.

CLANG-CLANG-CLANG-CLANG

Townsfolk and others from nearby homesteads poured down the hill toward the Malden Coal Mine. Bakersbee relied on the mine for employment and income, but it wasn't unusual for miners to get trapped in the narrow tunnels, or worse.

Scooter raced toward a group of men standing at the cavernous entrance. "Where's my pa?" he implored the miners. When no one met his gaze, his heart plummeted into his belly.

A gaunt-looking Mrs. Easterly, with an infant in her arms and twin girls clinging to her skirts, rushed up beside them. "What is it this time? My Charlie and both my boys are down there."

"What's happening?" Ma arrived with Hetty and Mary Malden.

The foreman, Luke Mulwatter, motioned for the boy to stop ringing the bell. "Listen, everyone," he said, holding both hands out to quiet the crowd. "The last group is on the way out, but tunnel three had a problem."

"They should've closed tunnel three last week when that rotted beam fell on Ben Tuten," Mrs. Easterly said.

Many nods and grunts of agreement from the people followed.

Is Pa in tunnel three?

"My George says it's not safe down there. We pray every morning to God for protection. Our seven kids need their pa," Liz Thompson, a small, thin woman, pleaded, a babe clutched in both arms. "If something happens to my man and he can't work, we'll be kicked out of the company house with nowhere to go."

"Hey!" Scooter shouted over the crowd. "How many are in there? Is Junior Wagner in there?"

"A team of eight men were in tunnel three," said Foreman Mulwatter.

"Give us names," several people demanded.

The crowd had swelled to at least thirty people—some townsfolk and the miners who'd made it out.

"Tell us who they are," urged Liz Thompson.

Scooter squared his shoulders to hear the answer.

"Junior Wagner is the team leader. With him were—I mean, are—Charlie Easterly, Chuck Easterly, David Easterly, Harry O'Connor, George Thompson, Abe Pickens, and Elias Carter. Junior knows what to do in a crisis, so let's assume he got them to a safe place."

"We need to get to them." Scooter spun and charged toward the entrance.

Ethan Thomas, the oldest miner in the group, caught his shoulder in a vice-like grip. "Not so fast, young'un. After the next group comes out, we'll make a chain and go after them," he said, turning toward the men. "Who's with me?"

Almost all the men circled closer, nodding their heads. No one wanted to be left behind in a tunnel, so everyone needed to pitch in to get the trapped workers out.

"The dust is thick from the cave-in, so cover your mouths with something," Ethan ordered.

Scooter had nothing to use, so he just waited with the rest.

"Take this," Mary said.

He swung his gaze to the petite brunette as she quickly detached the white cloth from her cloche hat.

"It's long. You can double it for better protection. Be careful," she whispered, her eyes bright with unshed tears.

"Thanks," he murmured.

Seven tired, dirty men shuffled out of the mine, and a few women rushed to meet them. Scooter was glad these men were okay, but he wished his father was among them.

Foreman Mulwatter said, "That's everyone except Junior's group. Make a human chain and bring the injured up by working together. You lot who just came up, take the top end."

"I'll go first," Scooter said.

"No, you won't, young'un. You never been in that mine. My crew is in front, and you can be number nine," Ethan Thomas said. "No more than ten feet between us and stay by the guide rope."

The mine had a deep entrance with the first thirty feet on a steep incline. Ropes were strung along both walls to make it easier for the men to climb up at the end of a shift, and the coal was brought up in a rail cart on a pulley system. The cart was large enough to hold six men, but the previous year, the pulley had failed, and an entire team had perished when the cart fell back down the incline. No one had chosen to ride in the bucket since then.

The sun dropped on the horizon, and the wind blew colder. Some women and children were crying, but no one would leave until the final eight were brought to the top. Scooter glanced back at his mother and

Hetty. Mary was still with them. He nodded and followed the man before him down into the tunnel.

Ethan led with a lantern in one hand and the other on the rope. Scooter wanted to rush past the slow-moving group, but he forced himself to stay in line as they walked down the rough dirt and stone. It finally leveled out at the bottom, but the dust made it difficult to see anything.

Ethan said, "The entrance to tunnel three is covered. I need five men on shovels and ore cars to put the dirt in."

The men around Scooter leaped into action, several backtracking to tunnel two to bring the ore cars down the track while others proceeded forward to begin the digging. He'd never been this deep in the earth, and he gasped for air. His heart pounded. For a minute, he sagged back against the wall behind him, praying for control. The air was thick with dust from the cave-in, and he could barely see his hand in front of his face.

"You'll be fine. Being down here takes some getting used to," said the miner closest to him before thrusting a shovel into Scooter's hands. "Go help with digging. Having something in your hands will help."

"Th-thanks," he stuttered, grabbing the short shovel and hurrying toward the sounds of digging ahead. Just as he reached the diggers, someone cheered.

"I hear Junior on the other side. Everyone quiet!" Ethan ordered.

Everyone stopped moving, and Scooter held his breath to listen.

"We're here," his pa said, coughing hard.

"Pa!" Scooter rushed forward, but Ethan stopped him again.

"Use your shovel and put the dirt in the ore car. We need to work fast in case there's another cave-in."

It took thirty minutes to bust a path through the debris, but soon the men pulled the missing eight through to the main tunnel. Only something was very wrong.

"What's that black stuff on your legs, Pa?" asked Scooter.

"When the top broke down, we tried to punch around it and hit a pocket of the stuff. If it were hot, I'd say we had a volcano, but it's a sticky moving mass like roof tar, and it kept coming. It's knee-high where we were trapped."

Ethan hunched over to look at Pa's legs. "I've never seen the like." He reached out to touch it, and Pa shoved his hand away.

"It's not safe to touch. Let's get out of here. This tar feels like it's eating at my skin," Pa said. "Chuck and David weren't wearing shoes, and it got them bad. They can't walk. Harry either."

Scooter grabbed a plank that had been pushed off to the side. "If we had a couple of these, two men could carry one out."

"Good thinking, son."

"Get David on this one, and we'll take him first," Ethan directed, organizing pairs of men to carry the three worst injured. The planks were too narrow to lie flat, but the men straddled them to keep the weight off their feet.

None of the eight looked good to Scooter, though three were worse off. All of them had sticky black tar halfway up their legs. Scooter fell in line, his pa in front of him as they made the slow shuffle walk back to the entrance.

At the steepest part, Ethan said, "We'll cart the boys up in the bucket first. I need four men on ropes. After we get them up, we'll follow with Harry in a second bucket. Who are my eight?"

Mary Malden couldn't believe her father's words.

"Do what I say, Mary. You don't need to be out here with these people." He lowered his voice. "This rabble isn't a place for a young lady."

"Papa." She scowled at the man she dearly loved, but who sometimes infuriated her. "There are men trapped down there. Scooter's father is trapped. I can't leave. Maybe we can help somehow."

"There is nothing you can do. The nurse is over there, and she'll do what she can."

"What if someone needs to go to the hospital?"

Papa gripped her arm and marched her away from the crowd toward the store. "It will be dark soon, and driving in these mountains at night isn't safe. These people are used to taking care of themselves. It's their way. Now I'll walk you to the hotel. You can have them bring you some warm milk to help you sleep."

She knew there was no point in arguing, but she had no intention of going to bed. Her mother had passed five years prior, and Mary was much more self-sufficient than her papa realized. Also, she wasn't the dutiful daughter he expected. She'd go to her room, and as soon as he left, she'd come right back here.

His pa was having trouble walking, and it got worse on the climb. Scooter put an arm around him, supporting his weight to the top.

"Junior!" His mother yelled, "I'm coming to you!"

Scooter got his pa over to the side before he collapsed with a groan. "Pa?"

The crowd fell silent, except for the Easterly boys sobbing in pain. Charlie Esterley had also fallen down by the cart.

"What's happening?" Reginald Malden demanded. "What's that stuff on the men?"

"Not sure, but nobody touches it. We need to wash it off," the foreman insisted.

Maude, the town nurse and the closest thing they had to a doctor since Dr. McMahan passed, rushed to the Easterly boys. "Someone needs to go to Doc's place and get a bottle of laudanum. Make that two."

"Where are your boots, Junior?" Ma asked.

Pa's feet were so black that Scooter hadn't realized he wasn't wearing boots.

"I gave them to Elias."

Then Reginald Malden was there. "You're the crew leader. Tell me what happened?"

"Sir, the beam gave way. We replaced the one that fell on Ben last week, but this was the other side. It fell, and we tried to hack into the side tunnel. We hit a pocket of this black sludge. It gushed out on top of us. We had rubble on both sides and no way to escape it. Stuff ate right through our clothes."

CHAPTER THREE

Everyone pitched in carrying buckets of water, but the sticky tar wasn't easy to wash off, and Pa kept asking to go home. He couldn't walk, so Scooter borrowed a cart. It was a small two-wheel cart, big enough for Pa to sit on the back and Scooter to pull it from the front.

"Hetty," Ma said, "run ahead and have your brothers, Laris and John, stoke the fire and put water on to heat. We have to wash this tar off your father as quick as we can."

Scooter's hands ached from holding the wood handles steady on the rough trail. Pa didn't complain; he lay there panting with his eyes closed.

"Did the laudanum Ms. Maude give him put him to sleep?" Scooter asked.

"I hope so," Ma said. "You'll need to go back to town for more as soon as we get him cleaned up.

"Yes, ma'am."

When they reached the cabin, all the kids were waiting in the yard. Nine-year-old John and ten-year-old Laris raced to help pull the cart to the porch stairs.

"I'll carry him inside," Scooter said.

"No, let's get his clothes off and try to wash his legs out here," Ma said. "No one touches the tar. When we're done, you boys get a shovel and bury his clothes and anything left."

It took the better part of an hour, and it was full dark when Ma was satisfied they'd gotten as much of the tar off as possible. With John's help, Scooter lifted Pa and carried him to the old rope bed his parents shared beneath the loft. The cabin had one other small room for the two girls. The five younger boys slept in the loft, while Scooter had a lean-to where he slept on the side of the cabin, except on the coldest nights, when he would curl up on the floor before the stove. They had little, but his family had love and looked after each other. Seeing his pa in pain broke his heart. All the kids were crying, but no one said much.

Scooter stroked his father's head while saying a prayer. *Is Pa going to die? What'll we do if he can't work? Lord, what'll happen to me? I don't want to work in the mine. Sorry, Lord, I don't mean to sound selfish. Please save my pa.*

"Scooter." Ma put a hand on his back, and he turned to hug her.

His breath hitched in a sob. "Ma, why does something this terrible have to happen?"

She held him away from her. "Be my strong man. Return the cart and find Nurse Maude. We'll need more laudanum before morning, and I need to know how to prevent infection. Ask around and see how the Easterly boys are doing. Your father will want to hear when he wakes up."

The hotel was actually a boarding house with three rooms to let, but it was clean, and Mrs. Jepson had a bowl of soup waiting for Mary and her papa in the kitchen. It seemed rude to refuse. Besides, she was hungry, so Mary sat at the table with her father and ate the thick vegetable stew in silence. When he was done, Papa gave her a nod.

"Go to bed. I'll see you in the morning."

"Goodnight, Papa," she said, kissing his cheek and hurrying to her room. She had to make him think she planned to obey, but she wouldn't just lay about and do nothing. After locking her door, she opened her bag to search for what she thought of as her medical kit.

She had been following Mrs. Kisselton around for the last few years, learning as much as possible when she wasn't away at school or attending boring dinners with her father. "I wish she was here now," she murmured.

The wise woman had given her a small supply of herbs for fever and pain besides the burn cream, in case Mary ever needed it when she wasn't home. She had a small amount of ground goldenseal and some white willow bark. The bark would have to be boiled, but it was a good fever and pain reducer. The goldenseal was better, but the dosing was tricky. She wondered if the nurse used natural remedies or only used laudanum.

She tucked the herbs in her reticule and pulled on a brown cloak with a hood. It was cold tonight, and she might have to stand around for a bit. Stepping into the hall, she hurried to the front, only to find Mrs. Jepson and her husband sitting by the door.

"No, Miss," Mr. Jepson said. "Your pa said you might try to go out, and we're to keep you here. It's no place for a lady out there."

"But maybe I can help," she implored.

"My son is a miner, but he made it out. We take care of our own in Bakersbee. Best you get on to bed," Mrs. Jepson said, bobbing her head firmly.

Mary wouldn't be able to get past these two, so she pretended obedience. "Okay. I'm tired, anyway." She feigned a yawn.

Two hours later, she paced the small room. The light was out, but there was still a light in the hall and her papa hadn't returned to the house. What was happening? She stared out the window, miserable about not knowing what had happened at the mine. *Lord, maybe I can't help, but I'd like to try. Please tell me what I should do.* No sooner had that prayer gone up than a full moon peeked out of the clouds, lighting up the night sky.

Mary took that as a sign and slipped on the cloak. She hung her reticule with her herbs on her wrist and climbed out the first-floor window. It didn't take long to skirt the buildings and get close to the mine.

Her father stood with the foreman and several other men, but most of the crowd had dispersed. She spun back and raced toward the old doctor's house. He was gone, but his nurse still saw patients there just as she had when he was alive.

She felt disappointed at the sight of the dark house. Was Nurse Maude at someone's house? Who was hurt?

"Mary, what are you doing here?"

She spun to find Scooter Wagner standing behind her. He was sweating, and his hair hung in disheveled waves on his forehead.

"How's your pa?" Mary squinted, trying to see him better in the dim light.

"Haven't you heard?"

She scowled. "No one tells a girl anything. Papa made me go to the boarding house, and they practically locked me in my room."

"You aren't there now."

She jerked her shoulder in a shrug. "I had a window."

He huffed and pushed past her to open the door to the doctor's house.

"I don't think Maude is here," Mary said, following him inside.

"I know. Saw her at the Easterly place. She told me where to find the laudanum for my pa." Scooter unlocked the desk drawer with a key he fished from his pocket. "She only has four bottles in here."

Mary leaned over his arm to see for herself. "Is your pa hurt?"

"Yes," he said with a shuddering breath. He took out two bottles before relocking the drawer. "I have to run one of these to the Easterly place and get home with the other for Pa. The men got poisoned by something from the earth. A black tar that ate away their skin. The pain is real bad."

"Oh no." Mary's heart pounded in her chest. "How can I help?"

He heaved a sigh and patted her shoulder awkwardly. "Thanks for checking. Checking on my pa."

She watched him jog away, then raced after him. "Wait. I have something to help."

Scooter turned back to her. "What do you mean?" he asked, his eyes wide.

She opened her reticule and pulled out the two small pouches. "This is goldenseal, and this is white willow bark. Does your mother have these?"

"I don't think so."

"Boil the bark. The goldenseal is strong, so you can't use much. Just a pinch in a cup of hot tea. See how he responds before you give him more. It's strong enough to stop a heart, so be careful. It's real good for pain and fever."

"How do you learn this?"

"The wise woman in Pinevale Valley taught me."

Scooter hesitated, then grabbed her hand and kissed the back. "Thank you," he said, then dashed out of sight between the buildings.

CHAPTER FOUR

Scooter detoured by the Easterly's place, running all the way, but it was still late when he returned home. All six kids were on the porch, and Scooter heard his father shouting inside.

"Helen, it's bad."

His father's anguish froze him in his tracks. The children were crying, and their voices combined sounded like a mournful wake for a funeral.

"Move," Scooter said, starting up the steps to the door. "I've got laudanum for Pa," he added breathlessly.

When he crossed to the bed, Pa's face was swollen

and his eyes red. He didn't seem to be aware of Scooter in the room. "Here's the medicine."

"It's more than I can stand, Lord. Take me home ..." moaned Pa.

Ma grabbed a spoon and, cradling Pa's chin, poured the sharp-smelling liquid into his mouth. "Swallow, Junior, it's for pain."

He moaned and thrashed but swallowed the dose.

They waited, watching him for a full five minutes before Ma gave him a second spoonful.

"Is that safe?"

"The pain is so great I'm feared for his heart," Ma said.

The second dose seemed to work. Pa's eyes went glassy, and he nodded off. Ma sank to the floor by the bed and put her face in her hands.

Scooter crouched beside her, not knowing how to help.

Her head snapped up. "Is Maude coming?"

"Not tonight. She's at the Easterly place. Those boys got burned real bad. They didn't have shoes."

"Neither did your pa, because the silly man gave them to Elias Carter. This is terrible." Tears dripped down her face, and her shoulders shook.

Scooter murmured, "Mary gave me something."

Ma wiped her cheeks with her apron, and he helped her to stand. "Mary Malden?"

"Yes. She says there's a wise woman who is a kind of doctor in Pinevale Valley. Mary helps her sometimes. Anyway, she gave me these." He pulled the two pouches from his pocket. For a minute, he couldn't remember which was which. "The bark. She called it white willow—"

"I think my mother used white willow for fever and pain. This is good." Ma held up the other bag. "And this?"

"She said you had to be real careful with that. It's called goldenseal. Mary said to just use a tiny pinch at first. It's stronger but good for pain and infection."

"Thank the Lord for Mary Malden. See if she can get more for us."

～

Scooter woke before dawn to the sound of Pa's voice through the cabin wall. He felt as though he hadn't slept at all after all the running, and he'd stayed up past one to help give Pa more laudanum. He rolled off his narrow cot and shook out his boots before sliding his feet into them. The lean-to gave him privacy from his siblings, and heat from the stove kept the worst of the chill out, but this time of year he slept fully dressed to stay warm.

"Helen," Pa called. "Where are you? The pain's returning. I need you."

By the time he got inside, Ma had already dosed him with laudanum.

Knock, knock.

Scooter rushed to the door to find an exhausted nurse Maude.

"Hello, Scooter. I'm checking on your pa."

"The laudanum helped him sleep."

"Yes, but it doesn't fix what's wrong." Maude shook her head sadly. "Can I see him?"

"This way."

Pa was drowsy while Maude checked him over and examined his legs and feet. Then she motioned for Scooter and Ma to converse with her a few feet away.

"He seems to have more on him than some others, and his feet look bad."

Ma crossed her arms. "Junior gave his boots to another man."

"I see." Maude pursed her lips. "If you have money, you must purchase some Epsom salt from the general store. It's magnesium sulfate, and if you soak his feet, it will help pull out the poison. You can also melt it in warm water and dip cloths to apply it to the skin. Beyond that, we have to wait and see if the poison spreads. I sent a telegram to Dr. Lancaster at the hospital in Ashville. He replied that, if it spreads, the best solution would be amputation."

"No!" Ma said. "That's a death sentence for him. He wouldn't be a man if he couldn't provide for our family."

"I'm sorry. That's what his telegram said. The doctor will come here in a day or two to see what can be done. I need to check on the others, but I'll try to come back tomorrow."

"Thank you," Ma said, before pulling a chair up to Pa's bed and taking his hand.

"I'll walk you out, Ms. Maude," Scooter said. "John and Laris are milking the cow, and I'd best help them."

"Scooter?" Pa asked weakly.

"Pa? I'm here." Hope rushed through him. Pa would be alright. "Don't worry. We're taking care of everything."

Pa grabbed his hand. "Son, I want you to sign up to work in the mine. This here's a company house, and if'n I can't work, we'll lose the cabin. It's all we got, so you got to go down and sign the papers."

The words were a punch to his gut. No, no, no. *The mine.* "Pa ... Please, no," Scooter begged. All these years doing odd jobs and running errands to prove it wouldn't be necessary for him to work in the mine and now it was going to happen anyway. "Pa, I can't. There are other things I want to do."

Pa's eyes were bright with fever. "Promise me you'll go sign the papers."

"I'll take care of the family," Scooter said. He hadn't said he'd sign the papers, but if it came to it and that was the only way, he would sign his soul to the darkness of the earth.

Then an idea flashed in his mind, a way that he could help Pa and the other injured men. He had to speak to Mary Malden.

~

Mary sat across from her papa at the table in Mrs. Jepson's house. She had a boiled egg and toast on her plate, but she wasn't hungry. She had to make him understand. "No, Papa."

"This is not up for discussion. I will work long hours with the dealings at the mine and can't spend time with you. The driver will take you back to Pinevale today and return for me in a couple of days. Mary, I'm sorry for being short with you last night. You're too young to be interested in the workings of the mine. I have handled all the details about helping the men. It's not a concern for you."

"But you will help them? The men who were injured and their families?" Mary asked hopefully.

Papa's jaw popped, and his mouth twisted in a flat line. "There are things you don't understand about business and employees—"

"Those men work for you, and they were injured. Are you going to provide a doctor for them? Pay them their wages while they heal?"

"Every mine employee is well-paid. They also sign a contract waiving their rights to compensation if they are unable to continue in the same capacity."

"That's not fair."

Papa shook his head. "Life isn't fair, and you're going home. That's final."

Tears burned her eyes, but she fought them back. "I want to see my friend Scooter before I leave town." She realized she'd made a grave error as soon as the words left her mouth. Her papa would never approve of such an association.

"Scooter?" He plopped his coffee cup back on the saucer. "Who exactly is Scooter?"

Mary sat up straighter. "His father is Junior Wagner."

Papa huffed out a breath. "The leader in tunnel three."

"Yes. I've known Scooter for years. We played together as children, and yesterday, I saw him at the store before the bell rang. We're friends."

"Friends. Aren't you old to be having male friends?"

Her cheeks flushed. Her thoughts about Scooter were not really those of a friend, but she couldn't let Papa know that. "I am not. It's 1926, and the world is changing."

Papa huffed. "Your mother would approve, no doubt." Then he sobered. "But she's gone, and I'm your remaining parent. I disapprove of male friends."

Knock, knock.

They both turned to see Scooter standing in the dining room doorway.

He held his knit cap in his hands. "Mrs. Jepson let me in."

"Scooter, how's your pa?" Mary crossed to him.

Her Papa got to his feet. "Scooter Wagner, since you're here, why don't you join us? We were discussing you, so your arrival is fortuitous."

Scooter licked his lips, and his eyes traveled over the table. "No, thank you, sir. I just needed to ask Mary something."

Papa crossed his arms. "She's here. Ask her now."

He shifted from foot to foot. "My pa is in a bad way, and so are the other men. What I'm saying is ... the nurse is all we have in Bakersbee, and she sent a telegram to Ashville. That doctor said they might have to amputate."

Mary's heart clenched in her chest. "Oh, no."

Scooter shook his head. "That would be the worst possible thing for my pa."

Her papa heaved a long sigh. "Your father and the men had contracts with Malden Mines. I'm not responsible for accidents—"

Scooter looked from Mary to her father and tipped up his chin. "I don't know about any contracts, but I want to go to Pinevale Valley with Mary and speak with Mrs. Kisselton. See if she can help. The willow bark tea and goldenseal already worked wonders. Pa could talk real good this morning and the pain was less."

"That's a great idea." Mary circled the table and clutched Papa's sleeve. "You want me to go home today, anyway. I'll go without a fuss if Scooter can ride with me. Then the driver can bring him back when he returns for you."

"You think I'd let you two ride together—"

"Papa," she interrupted. "The driver would be with us, and Scooter can sit up front with him. Please. Mrs. Kisselton can help them, I'm sure of it. Or you could pay to transport all the men to the hospital in Ashville. That would be the humane thing to do, contract or no contract."

Scooter edged farther into the room. "The doctor in Asheville talked about amputation. They wouldn't want to go there. Somewhere else or bringing Mrs. Kisselton here would be better."

Papa's mouth flattened in a straight line, and he glared at her.

But he was coming around. Deep down, her father was a compassionate man. It was just ... buried deep.

His brows furrowed. "Fine. I'll agree for the sake of the employees. Although there is no guarantee Isobel Kisselton will travel here. It's a ten-hour trip by car. Days in that wagon of hers. Since I'm allowing this young man to travel with you, you won't be staying over anywhere. You will drive straight through. It will be a long, hard drive."

"Yes, Papa, thank you!" She threw her arms around him.

He patted her awkwardly on the back. "I'll speak to my driver. You should leave right after breakfast."

"Thank you, sir." Scooter spoke up.

She glanced over to see his face split in a wide grin. She couldn't help smiling right back into his blue eyes.

"You behave yourself with my daughter," Papa said.

Scooter tugged on his cap. "God bless you, Mr. Malden. I need to tell Ma, so she won't look for me. If I run all the way, I'll be back in less than an hour."

CHAPTER FIVE

Scooter ran back to town, and when he got to the mercantile where Mr. Malden's Packard was waiting, he had to bend over and catch his breath.

Mary rushed toward him. "Scooter! I was getting worried. Do you need some water? Papa, he needs some water."

"Mary, you run inside and get two more glass bottles of water for the trip. Two water jugs are in the trunk, but having a bottle would be easier. Gerald, did you top off the auxiliary tank, so you have enough gas for the entire trip? I want you to drive straight through to Pinevale Valley. Drop the boy with Mrs. Kisselton and take Mary home."

"Yes, sir, Mr. Malden." A tall, big-boned man with laugh lines around his eyes stood in a black uniform by the Packard. "When do I return to bring you home?"

"The boy will try to convince Mrs. Kisselton to return with you to see about the injured men. I suggest you rest a day and service the car. You can make the return trip the day after. Bring Scooter back with or without Mrs. Kisselton. This is December, and the weather could change at any time. I don't want to get stranded in Bakersbee if I can help it, but my business here will last a few days."

"Yes, sir."

Mr. Malden handed him some folded bills. "Here's some extra cash for emergencies and to fill the tanks before you return. If you need anything else, see the estate manager. And Gerald, this is Scooter Wagner." He turned to Scooter. "Young man, you do whatever Gerald tells you to do, understood?"

"Yes. Yes, sir." Scooter had finally caught his breath and stood up straight, adjusting his bag.

Mr. Malden looked him up and down. Scooter fidgeted under his scrutiny. He'd run by Liam

McCord's house to borrow a vest and a hat. Liam's wife Millie had insisted he take her small carpetbag, a fresh loaf of bread, and a jar of jam. There hadn't been time to pack anything else.

"Listen to me." Mr. Malden gripped Scooter's upper arm and leaned in close, his gray eyes boring into him. "I need you to heed what I'm about to tell you."

"Yes, sir." Scooter nodded vigorously.

"You are to be polite to my daughter, but at no time will you be familiar with her person. Am I understood?"

"I wouldn't dream, sir—"

Mr. Malden interrupted him. "Your family lives in company housing. If you so much as touch my daughter or play with her affections, you will find your family looking for new accommodations. Have I made myself clear?"

"Yes, sir." Scooter wasn't good enough for Mary, but all the same, his heart crumpled a little in his chest. She was special, but not for him.

"Good. We have an understanding."

"I have the water!" Mary said, running down the steps with two large glass bottles.

Scooter stepped forward to take them and froze in his tracks, glancing at Mr. Malden. The man gave a quick nod, and Scooter accepted the bottles. "Let me help," he said.

Mr. Malden opened a back door. "Mary, you ride in the back. You have your books and a nice warm blanket. If it gets too hot, you can crank a window down but lower the curtain to keep down the dust.

"Yes, Papa." She kissed his cheek. "I have the maps, too, and I'll help with navigating like I did on the way here."

"My beautiful girl." Malden shut her door and glared at Scooter and Gerald. "Both of you are to protect her with your life."

"Yes, sir," Scooter said.

"Of course, sir," said Gerald.

It was time to go. Scooter looked at the shiny handle on the gray door of the Packard 8. Everything was terrible right now, with Pa and the men injured, but he was going to ride in an actual car. He climbed into the passenger side and waited for Gerald to get situated.

Gerald was well over six feet, with very tan skin, deep chestnut hair, and thick muscular arms. Of course, driving a car on these dirt roads was a difficult and physically demanding job.

"Have you ever ridden in a car?" Gerald asked.

"No, sir. Do I need to crank it?"

"Nope, the Packard has an electric starter button. We have the hand crank for emergencies, but it's unnecessary right now. Watch this: I set the hand brake like this, then adjust the spark and throttle levers on the steering wheel and press this button."

The car jolted to life.

∼

Mary couldn't believe her father had let Scooter ride in the car with her. Right until they drove out of the mountain pass, she'd thought he'd change his mind and either make her stay or Scooter go back to his house. She turned around to peek at the buildings as they disappeared in the distance. After the first rest stop, she'd try to talk Scooter into riding in the back with her.

It was hard to be heard over the seats because of the engine noise and the creaking of the car as they drove the dirt road. On the other side of the mountain range, when they got into North Carolina, the roads would be graveled in places, but closer to Pinevale, there were more dirt roads.

She loved her hometown. It had the most magnificent fountain right in the center. Leaning forward, she rested her chin on her hands on the back of the front seat. "Scooter, did I tell you we have an enormous fountain in the middle of town?"

"A fountain?" He turned his head, and their faces were so close that she saw tiny gold flecks in his green eyes.

"Yes. Water from a natural spring powers it, and the basin is set with thousands of colorful rocks. It makes the water change colors at different times of the day."

He coughed and cleared his throat. "That's sounds very nice."

"Oh, I forgot to give you a cup." She pulled a metal cup from the basket on the floor. "You can keep that one for the trip. Gerald, Papa said we had to drive straight through. Do you think we'll get there before dark?"

"I hope so, young miss, but you have extra blankets back there. The temperature will drop when the sun goes down, so we'll only take brief rest stops. Your papa had Mrs. Jepson at the hotel pack a lunch bag. It's in the trunk. We must stop every three hours and rest the engine for thirty minutes."

She glanced at Scooter again, but he was staring straight ahead. "Scooter, did you bring a jacket?" she asked.

"No. I have my wool shirt, though. I'll be fine with that."

She frowned and relaxed back in her seat. Why wasn't he talking to her? He was probably worried about his pa.

∾

Scooter knew Mary wanted him to chat with her, but her father's words rang like a klaxon in his skull. If he thought Scooter had been familiar with Mary, he might kick Scooter's entire family out of the company's housing.

Would it happen anyway, if his pa was unable to work? Scooter heaved a long sigh. This was his first chance to ride in a car, but the dread of that future kept him enjoying the ride. He would most likely have to work in the mines when this was over. He'd have to accept that fact.

An hour passed in silence. Scooter watched Gerald steer the car on the rough roads. He was a skillful driver.

"Is driving hard?" Scooter asked, a big yawn slipping out. He hadn't slept since the night before last.

Gerald shrugged. "The road is washed out in places, and we have to avoid the worst spots or change a tire before lunch. We only have one spare."

"Mary said it's two hundred and sixty miles. If I had a horse and cart, I reckon it'd take me two weeks to get there."

"Yes," Gerald said with a nod. "It's kind of Mr. Malden to allow you to use the car to bring back Mrs. Kisselton."

"I'm thankful. It's an answer to prayer," Scooter said quietly. "My pa doesn't have a month to wait for help to arrive. Only we don't know if Mrs. Kisselton will return to Bakersbee." It was that unknown that scared him. He wished he knew more about her.

He turned on the seat and saw Mary looking at him with big blue eyes. She was so beautiful that his tongue got tangled in his throat for a second, and he just stared at her.

"What?" she asked.

"Mrs. Kisselton. Do you think she'll help us?"

Mary leaned up on the seat back again. "She's a good person. When people who can't afford to pay come to her, she helps them anyway. Says that's her calling in life to take care of folks." She paused, her mouth a flat line. "Mrs. Kisselton's mother was a Cherokee Indian, and her family on that side still lives in the Qualla Boundary."

"I read about that in school. That's the Indian reservation?"

"Yes. It's about seventy-five miles from Pinevale Valley. The Cherokee own that land. They are citizens now, too, as of four years ago. You aren't going to have a problem with her being an Indian, are you? She's a great—"

He interrupted before she got wound up. "No, Mary. My ma raised me to see all people as God's children. We are all equally important to God, so we are equal here on earth."

Gerald nodded in satisfaction at those words. That's when Scooter realized Gerald wasn't just tan. He also had high cheekbones and dark black hair.

Scooter turned his head to peer at Mary again. "Will Mr. Kisselton let her come back with us to Bakersbee?" His pa would never allow his mother to travel without him.

"Her husband died a few years ago, though she has a son. He's twelve, and his name is Wally." Mary put a hand on Scooter's shoulder. "I wouldn't have told you to come if I didn't think she'd help. She might not go to Bakersbee, but she'll give you medicine. I'm sure of it."

He had exactly seventy-eight cents in his pocket. There'd been no time to dig up the four dollars he had buried in a jar by the creek for emergencies. This would've qualified as a dire emergency, but he'd been so busy running home and to Mr. Liam McCord's house that he forgot to get it.

"Maybe if she'll come with us now, I can go back and work for her to pay her back for her help."

If I can stay out of the mine.

The road improved in the cities, and one hour dissolved into the next. At the three-hour mark, Gerald stopped the car to add water and check all the lines. They ate the sandwiches from Mrs. Jepson's basket. Scooter wolfed down two without a thought and then realized they were probably supposed to last until supper.

"Sorry. Did I eat too much?" he asked Gerald.

The big man flashed him a smile. "It will be fine. There's a little community called Ambrose on the other side of Black Mountain. I know a safe place to stop to eat, and I can fill up the tank."

Mary came back from doing her business behind a tree. "I feel like running up and down the road to stretch my legs."

"No time, young miss. We're ready to go."

Three hours later, they stopped again to stretch and check the car. Scooter shared his bread and jelly from Millie McCord.

"Tell me who Millie McCord is again?" Mary asked. "You mentioned them earlier, and I didn't have a chance to ask."

"Mr. Liam McCord is a great man from England." Scooter added more of the sweet jam to his slice of bread. "He moved here and lived by himself up in the mountains for a long time. Then, by a miracle, he saved a young woman's life, and she was hurt, so Millie helped take care of her."

"Is Millie his wife?"

"She is now, and they are expecting a baby. That's why Millie wasn't helping with the injured. Liam didn't want her risking herself. She's Maude's sister and knows a little about nursing."

"Does the young woman live with them?"

"No, she got her memory back and went home to her family. I'll—"

"Young'uns," Gerald interrupted. "The story is interesting, but we need to get back on the road. Save it for another day."

They gathered up their trash and set off again in the car. The noise of the engine and the tires on the rough road made talking difficult while they drove. Scooter kept thinking of things he'd like to tell Mary, to hear her voice. But then ... what if Gerald reported they were getting too close to Mr. Malden?

Scooter blew out a breath and tried to get comfortable in the jouncing seat. He needed to keep his distance from Mary Malden. For his family's sake.

Finally, they stopped for supper in the little community of Ambrose. Scooter climbed out and opened Mary's door. She stuck her hand out, and he gripped her fingers to pull her out of the car. When her bare hand touched his, it felt like a jolt of energy touching her fingers.

If only things were different.

"Do you have money to eat, young man?" Gerald's words yanked his gaze from Mary.

"Ah ... No, sir. Not for food." He had seventy-eight cents, but he might need that to pay Mrs. Kisselton.

"Fine, then. You wait in the car, and we'll bring you back any leftovers she gives us."

"No." Mary crossed her arms.

"Miss, please understand. Mr. Malden didn't give me money to waste on this young man. He allowed money for the two of us." He dipped his head, and the corners of his mouth turned up. "Don't you worry. Mrs. Keen will undoubtedly have something we can bring for your ... young Scooter."

CHAPTER SIX

For Scooter, the last three hours of the drive seemed the longest. He was worried about his pa, and the temperature dropped when the sun went down at five. It was so cold in the car that his teeth were chattering, and his toes felt numb even with the blanket Mary had given him.

They were all cold. Scooter glanced over the seat. Mary's face was all he could see in the cocoon of blankets, and her eyes were closed. He was too cold to sleep.

At just after eight o'clock, they drove through the tiny town of Pinevale Valley.

"Have you thought about where you'll sleep tonight?" Gerald asked him.

Scooter shook his head. "I thought I'd sleep in the car. I didn't realize it would be this cold."

"You'd freeze."

"He can stay at the house; we have half a dozen empty guest rooms," Mary offered from the back.

"No, Miss," Gerald said.

"No." Scooter said at the same time.

Gerald glanced at him. "Mr. Malden said to take you straight to Mrs. Kisselton, but that hardly seems right this late."

"Could I sleep in your barn?" Scooter asked hopefully.

"That's too cold!" Mary fussed.

"You can sleep on the floor in my kitchen," Gerald said. "My wife passed on last year, so you won't bother anyone."

"Th-thank you," he said through his chattering teeth.

"I'll insist on one thing, though." Gerald's gaze caught his. "Before we drive back the day after tomorrow, you'll take yourself down to the barbershop and have a bath."

Heat suffused Scooter's cheeks. He'd had a bath on Saturday, but with all the running and sweating—and today was Tuesday—he probably smelled ripe. He had no clean clothes, but he'd spend a nickel and get a bath if he had to. "I can do that, but where does Mrs. Kisselton live? I need to go see her first thing tomorrow."

"I'll show you the way," Mary volunteered.

Gerald shook his head. "No need, young miss. I'm sure you'll have your studies to attend."

Mary leaned forward and put her hands on the seat. "Mrs. Kisselton is my friend. I'll go over there whether you drive me or I take my pony."

~

The next morning, Gerald handed Scooter a large wedge of jerky. "No time for a hot meal. Wash up the best you can at the pump, and let's get over to Mrs. Kisseltons."

"Yes, sir." Scooter folded up the blanket he'd slept on and hurried to the outhouse to do his business.

When he returned to the front of Gerald's house, Mary stood there with her hands on her hips, obviously fussing with Gerald.

"Miss—"

"I'm going. Either in your car or on my pony."

Gerald gave him a sour look. "Get in the car then, and make sure you tell your papa I was against this. I don't want to lose my job."

Mary climbed in the back, and he and Gerald entered the front. The car revved to life, and they drove silently to Mrs. Kisselton's cabin.

The log house had a wraparound porch and wide front steps. At least a dozen hanging baskets and clay pots lined the porch. A plowed area lay to the side of the cabin and a small barn beyond that.

When they arrived, a boy was watering the plants. He put down his can and rushed inside. Moments later, the door opened, and a tall woman with dark skin and even darker hair in two long braids stepped onto the porch with the boy behind her. The resemblance between the pair was easy to see.

Mary whispered out of the side of her mouth. "That's her and her son, Wally."

Scooter walked to the foot of the stairs. "Hello, ma'am. My name's Scooter Wagner, and we've come a long way to ask you for help. There was a mine accident in Bakersbee, and my pa was hurt badly. Seven other men, too. Mary had some herbs you gave her. We don't have a doctor, and we were hoping you might help us. Please." The exhaustion from the past few days washed over him, and he thought he might break down in tears on this woman's porch.

Mrs. Kisselton's face softened, and she gestured behind her. "Come inside, all of you. I'll fix us tea, and you can tell me everything." Then she turned and walked inside without a backward glance, the boy on her heels.

Mary moved up beside him and grasped his hand. "She'll help, I know she will."

He shouldn't hold Mary's hand, but he couldn't bring himself to shake her off—even though Gerald might see. But he was so nervous, and having that connection with her felt good, if only for a few minutes.

"Sit, and I'll bring the tea," said Mrs. Kisselton.

There was a long wooden table with benches and chairs at the ends. Scooter sat on one side, and Mary slid in beside him without releasing his fingers. Gerald took a chair on the end.

Mrs. Kisselton said, "Wahyah, get the cups for everyone."

"I thought his name was Wally?" Scooter whispered to Mary.

The boy answered. His voice was deep, and his dark eyes were thoughtful as he placed five mugs on the table. "My name is Armand Wahyah. Most people call me Wally. Wahyah is my Cherokee name, and my father's name was Armand. He was French and was born in New Orleans. One day, I plan to visit there."

Gerald chuckled. "Young wolf, then. Do you have coffee or only tea?"

"Only tea." Mrs Kisselton brought a pot from the

stove to fill the mugs. "You'll like it. Mary, is this your young man?"

He tried to pull away. She only tightened her hold.

"Scooter is my friend, but I told him he should come here to ask for your help. You said once that it was a healer's divine privilege to help those in need. Will you help?"

Mrs. Kisselton took the seat at the end of the table. "Scooter, tell me about your father and this accident."

It didn't take long for him to tell her everything—the cave-in, the mysterious black tar, and how it had hurt the men. When he finished, they waited silently for her response.

She sipped her tea and studied each of them.

Scooter cleared his throat. "One more thing."

"Yes?" Her dark brows arched.

"I don't have money. I was going to offer to work for you. Maybe tend your gardens or whatever you needed to pay you for helping my pa and the others." He hesitated, the words burning his gut. "Only now I can't."

She waited, watching him with those dark eyes, and he felt compelled to continue.

"I can't because my dad is sick. The foreman says I've got to work the mines for our family to keep the company house. We probably shouldn't have bothered you, since we can't pay you."

She tilted her head, her mouth pursed. "Did Mary tell you I'm a doctor? Because I am merely an herbalist with knowledge passed down through my family for generations."

"She told me you were wise—a wise woman. And the things you gave Mary have already helped my pa. We need more for the other men."

"My talent is God given. The Lord brought you to my home, so I believe He wants me to help you as much as I'm able."

Scooter felt like leaping for joy. "Thank—"

"You must understand I am making no guarantees, but I'll do my best for your father and the rest."

"That's all we ask," Mary said.

"Good. Finish your tea, and we'll get to work. When do we return to Bakersbee?"

Gerald cleared his throat. "Tomorrow. I'll bring the car around at six to pick up Scooter, and you, if you're willing to return with us. Mr. Malden is staying a few more days, so you'd ride back here to Pinevale with us when his business is completed."

"Well then, we have much work to do to prepare. I'll need all—"

Gerald interrupted. "Ma'am, I have to service the car, so I can't help you here."

"I have these two young people to help me. You too, Wahyah."

~

Scooter woke up early, washed his face in the basin by the outdoor pump, and put on the fresh shirt Mrs. Kisselton had given him. At least his shirt was clean, even if he hadn't had time to take a proper bath. Last night, Gerald had come to take Mary home at dark. Meanwhile, Scooter and Mrs. Kisselton had worked through the night, boxing the supplies and figuring out how much they could take back in the car to Bakersbee.

"Would you like some tea?" she asked when he came back inside.

"Yes, ma'am. Do we have everything ready?"

"Let's see. I finished the tinctures last night and bottled them up an hour ago—eight bottles for the eight men—and I proportioned out some items in separate boxes for each of the five households we'll visit. I'm going to need your help."

"I'm so grateful—"

"Hello!" The door burst open, and Mary came in with a basket over one arm.

"Mary." Scooter's breath caught. She wore the same hat she'd had in Bakersbee, this time with a bright red ribbon. "Why are you here?"

"What do you mean? I'm going with you, of course."

"Your pa—"

"He isn't here, is he? I'll ride in the back with Mrs. Kisselton. I only have a small bag, which won't take up much room. I want to help," Mary insisted.

Mrs. Kisselton nodded. "If this is where you need to be, join us."

"What about her pa?" If they went back together, he was bound to think Scooter hadn't kept his word. He knew Mary liked him, and he was head over heels in love with her, but that wasn't something anyone else could find out.

Mrs. Kisselton tilted her head, looking from one to the other. "Her pa isn't here, and if he didn't specifically forbid her to return, I won't interfere."

Scooter spun to glare at Mary. "Did he?"

"No." Mary flounced over to the table and whipped the napkin off her basket. "I have a basket of muffins and ham sandwiches beneath it, so that will be breakfast and lunch."

"Thank you, Mary," Mrs. Kisselton said.

A horn honked outside.

"It's time to go. Everyone grab a box, and let's load the car as quickly as possible," Mrs. Kisselton said.

Gerald balked at taking Mary back to Bakersbee with them, but it was three to one, so he finally agreed. After loading the many bags and boxes of healing items, there was barely room for Mary and Mrs. Kisselton in the back. Mrs. Kisselton's son,

Wally, hugged her goodbye and promised to watch over the plants and animals.

"Are you worried about your son being here alone?" Mary asked.

"Wally is a resourceful boy. He'll be fine," Mrs. Kisselton said. "I think I'll sleep all the way there."

Mary laughed. "Have you ridden across the country in an automobile? It's not an easy ride."

CHAPTER SEVEN

Scooter was grateful when Gerald agreed to drive them straight to his family's cabin late that evening. It had been a long, arduous trip, with only a few stops, but they'd made it back in less time than it'd taken to get to Pinevale Valley.

When they pulled up, no one was in the yard. Scooter's heart pounded in his chest. Had he been gone too long? Had Pa?

"Don't assume the worst young scamp," Gerald said.

"I need to go inside and check. Do we unload everything here first?" asked Scooter.

Gerald shook his head. "There are too many items to carry easily from house to house. I'll leave you with what you need and go home and change. I'll return before dawn to take you to the next house."

Mrs. Kisselton nodded. "Thank you, Gerald. That is most kind of you. We have five houses to attend tomorrow, and the automobile will help."

As he waited for them to get out of the car and Mrs. Kisselton to pick out what she needed, Scooter barely contained his agitation. Finally, he couldn't wait any longer. "I should go inside and see what's happening." He rushed up the steps to burst inside. "I'm home. And Mrs. Kisselton came back with us to help Pa," Scooter exclaimed.

Ma hurried forward to pull him into her arms. "My Scooter. I've been so worried."

"I'm fine, Ma. Where are the kids?"

"I sent them out to Liam and Millie's for a few nights. Pa's ... yelling has taken a toll on them."

"Hello, Mrs. Wagner," Mary said from behind him.

Ma reached past him to pull Mary into a hug. "Sweet girl. Thank you for helping my Junior."

Mary hugged her back, then bounced on her toes in

excitement. "We've brought Mrs. Kisselton." She half turned to allow his ma to see the wise woman.

Ma greeted Mrs. Kisselton with an extended hand. "We were about to give up hope. Are you a doctor, then?"

Mrs. Kisselton gave one of her mysterious half-smiles and tilted her head. "I'm not a doctor, but I'll do my best with the gifts and knowledge God has given me to help your husband and the other men."

"Ma!" Pa called out. "I can't stand the pain. Bring me laudanum."

Scooter raced across the cabin. "Pa, I'm back, and we have help."

Junior paused his thrashing and turned fevered eyes on him. "Scooter?"

"I'm not sure about this." Ma stood between Mrs. Kisselton and the bed.

Pa wailed again. "Ma! Help me!"

Scooter grasped Ma's arm. "What choice is there? Let her try."

"Please, Mrs. Wagner," whispered Mary. "If you let her help your husband, then the other women will let her help their men. It's the only way they'll let a stranger in their homes."

Pa moaned again.

Tears rolling down her cheeks, Ma stepped back and gestured for Mrs. Kisselton to proceed.

First, she opened the small satchel around her shoulder and pulled out a glass container. It was the tincture he'd helped her create and sweeten with honey.

Ma frowned. "What is that?"

"It's okay, Ma. I helped her make it. Mrs. Kisselton knows everything about herbs and plants. It will help."

She uncapped the bottle for Ma to smell. "I've found that turmeric helps to cleanse the bad things inside a person's body. A small amount of cloves helps relieve pain, and I added other herbs to encourage healing and balance in his body. Mostly, this is for the pain. The honey it's mixed with makes it taste better, but it will also relax him while fighting bacteria. You'll need to give him two teaspoons every hour for a day or two."

"When it runs out?" Ma asked.

"The ingredients are easy to procure for the most part. I'll give you the recipe and the items you might have difficulty finding. You give your husband two spoonfuls now, and we'll wait a few minutes before I check his legs."

After Pa drank some of the mixture, his eyelids drooped again.

"That's amazing," Ma said.

"Laudanum is something ... the body gets used to. This is important. You'll need to give him more laudanum before bed and in the morning for the next two days, or his body will crave it. He will get sick in a different way if you take it away all at once."

"I understand."

She nodded. "Since he is resting, let's have a look at his feet."

His ma and Mrs. Kisselton lifted the blanket and gently uncovered Pa's feet. They were red and swollen with big white splotches. "That looks bad," Scooter whispered.

"Shh," Mrs. Kisselton said. "We are not negative in the sick room. Scooter, retrieve the big cloth bag from the car and place it on the table. We only need that and one of the crates from the trunk, then Mr. Gerald can get some rest. Thank you, Gerald."

"Yes, ma'am." Gerald followed Scooter quickly outside.

"Mrs. Wagner, would you be so kind as to boil water for me? I need a large bowl with very hot water. I'll show you how to make a poultice from goldenseal and yarrow. You should have that on the mountains. I've shown Scooter what the plant looks like to make it easy for him to find."

"Just those?"

"No, I also have some blackberry root and black cohosh, but I brought enough of that with me to leave you some."

Scooter returned with the box and set to work laying the items out on the table.

Mrs. Kisselton continued. "Scooter described the black sludge to me, and although I've never seen anything like that, if it came from the earth's bowels, it most likely was highly acidic. We need to be certain there is no trace of it left. What did you wash his feet with?"

"I used water, but the soap was too harsh. I got the Epsom salt and made a poultice with it."

She smiled and patted Ma's arm. "That's excellent. You have done very well."

Ma looked so relieved that Scooter thought she might collapse, so he pulled a chair close behind her.

They spent the next few hours with Mrs. Kisselton, who instructed Ma on how to make the poultices and showed her how to apply them. Ma helped by raising Pa's feet so Mrs. Kisselton could wrap the soft cloth with the mixture around them, covering the top and bottom and going up his ankles, where the burns had blistered.

"The poultice should stay on his feet for six hours, then remove it so air can reach the sores for one to two hours before reapplying a new poultice. Lord willing, you'll see a difference in a couple of days.

When the burned areas degenerate into an ulcer patch and become difficult to heal because of the damaged flesh, use a muslin cloth with olive or sweet oil on his legs."

∽

Mary insisted on helping as they went from house to house, checking on the injured. Mrs. Kisselton was the epitome of grace. Two of the wives didn't want to let her in the house on account of her Indian hair, but Mary scolded them for their prejudice and reminded them we are all God's children.

By the end of the day, Mary was as exhausted as she'd ever been. Gerald pulled the car up to the Easterly cabin, and she climbed in the back. Most of the supplies had been distributed, so there was more room. She slid over to the far side, and to her surprise and delight, Scooter joined her.

She shifted closer and reached for his hand, but he pulled back.

"Mary, I can't."

"Can't what?"

"Ah ..." he said, glancing at the porch where Mrs. Kisselton and Gerald were speaking with Mrs. Easterly. "I just want to tell you I wish things were different, but they aren't. Please tell your pa we are only friends if he asks."

She was confused. "We are friends ... but ..." Why was he saying this? Unless ... "Did Papa say something to you? Something about me?"

"Mary ... I-I care about you, but we are not the same. You'll return to your fancy house, and I'll go down into the mines. I think it would be best if we kept our distance. I'm sorry." Then he slid out of the car and climbed into the front seat.

Mary wanted to weep. Had he just told her he cared about her, but they couldn't even be friends? Why had he said that? They were already friends, but she felt so much more for him.

∽

The following two days were a blur, with the routine based on Pa's pains and demands. As his feet and legs improved, his attitude became brittle. He wanted more, faster healing, less medication, Ma's attention, and Scooter to go to the mine.

Scooter divided his time between helping Pa and going with Mrs. Kisselton to the other five homesteads. He'd grown confident blending the ingredients, and she even sent him to check on the patients. He found he loved learning this new skill. The idea of helping people, maybe one day being a physician, and helping his community took root in his heart. He was so busy learning and working that he didn't have time to think about Mary. He tried not to mourn the loss of their friendship. She'd never forgive him for how he'd spoken to her, but he had to protect his family.

Gerald stopped by to tell Mrs. Kisselton they were leaving at seven sharp the next day for Pinevale Valley.

"How will we make it without you?" Ma asked her.

Mrs. Kisselton pulled his ma into a hug. "You'll be just fine. I've done all I can, and Scooter knows what to do almost as well as me now."

Pa was sitting up now, a blanket behind him to let him lean on the headboard. "Son, we'll lose our cabin if you don't go to work. I'm better, but not well enough to work. Do your duty as the oldest son and sign up at the mine."

This was Scooter's biggest nightmare—going down into the earth and working the mine. It was killing his pa in slow increments, and he didn't want that same fate. He wanted to learn more from Mrs. Kisselton and return that knowledge to help Bakersbee. "Pa. If I return to Pinevale Valley, I could study the plants with her, so I can help our people."

"Or go to medical school," Mrs. Kisselton said quietly.

"Don't be puttin' no ideas in my boy's head. We got no money for schoolin'. He needs to work like everyone else in this town."

Knock, knock.

Scooter opened the front door to find the foreman, Luke Mulwatter, on the porch.

"I've come to see your pa," said Mulwatter.

Nodding, Scooter led him to the bed beneath the stairs, where Ma was changing the poultices. She froze when she saw the foreman.

Mulwatter nodded a greeting. "Junior, Mrs. Wagner. It's good to see you both. I've heard you're getting better and that you won't lose your feet. That's good news."

Ma moved the muslin cloths to show him the blisters on Pa's legs.

"Mrs. Kisselton told us to expect the blisters, but they'll disappear in a few weeks. His legs are much better, and he's resting without the laudanum," Ma said.

"That's good to hear. I've checked in with three of the other men, and they will return to work the first of the week. The Easterly boys will take longer, but their pa says he's ready to work. Will you be back in the tunnel on Monday?"

"What?" Scooter bellowed. "Pa almost died."

"Enough, son." Pa scowled at him before turning back to the foreman. "I'll do my best, but I might need another week."

Luke made a clicking sound in his throat. Reluctant to meet their eyes, he said, "We miss your years of experience, but we have rules regarding our positions. This is a company cabin; someone must be at work Monday if your family wants to stay here."

"Scooter is fifteen. He's old enough to join the crews," Junior said.

"Good. See you Monday, Scooter." Mulwatter nodded, still not making eye contact, and left the house.

Scooter threw himself onto the edge of the bed. "Please, Pa, don't make me do this. I'll find another cabin for us, even work day and night to pay for it. I can't go into the mine."

With tears in her eyes, Ma quietly said, "There is no choice. Think about your brothers and sisters. It's the middle of December. You've got to go."

CHAPTER EIGHT

They were leaving for Pinevale Valley in the morning, and Mary didn't want to wait to speak with her father. Something had to be done for these poor mining families, and she would force him to see reason. Even if Scooter didn't love her, she wouldn't let him be sentenced to a lifetime in the mines to save his family home.

It wasn't fair. His family shouldn't be punished for something that happened in the mine. She raised her hand to knock on the door to Papa's room at the boarding house, but hesitated when she heard raised voices on the other side. Who was here at this time of night? It was after nine. Curiosity had her cracking the door open just enough to hear the conversation.

Papa snapped, "Why are you bringing this up now?"

"Sir, if it gets out that we knew something was amiss in that tunnel, it would be bad for the image of Malden Mines." She recognized the voice of Papa's foreman, Luke Mulwatter.

"You're supposed to handle these things. That's why you're the foreman."

"We can still keep it quiet. If we pay off the inspector, he won't tell anyone."

"Tell them what? We thought there might be a weak wall in that tunnel? That black tar was unheard of and hopefully will never be seen again in our lifetime," Papa said.

"But the fact remains that the inspection showed the wall had a weakness."

Mary's heart pounded, drowning out the rest of Mulwatter's words. Papa knew? The miners were hurt, and this whole time, Papa and his foreman covered up the fact that they knew the wall was weak.

She shoved the door open so hard that it hit the wall with a thump. "You knew?"

Papa jerked to his feet, and Mr. Mulwatter spun to face her.

"Why aren't you in bed?" Papa shouted.

Mary pointed at him, then Mulwatter, and then back at him. "I heard everything."

Papa covered his eyes with one hand. "You—"

"No. I'm no longer a child. I understood exactly what Mr. Mulwatter said. You have to take responsibility for those injured men."

"Mary, Mary. You don't understand. How could I—"

She interrupted. "Let them keep their cabins and guarantee full pay until February. Then, if they are better and want to work, give them back their jobs. If they aren't better, you won't be turning them out in the middle of winter." She crossed her arms and held her breath. If he agreed, the families of all those men would be saved. And Scooter. He would be saved from a life in the mines.

Her papa took a long breath. "Perhaps my daughter has more wisdom than either of us, Luke. Instead of covering up this mess, we should make reparations."

"Sir?"

"We are going to make this right. First, tunnel three is permanently closed. We will dig on the west side of the tunnel. Second, we will allow the injured men up to two months to recover with full pay. We'll call it compensation for work injury."

"We have to be careful how we word it," Mulwatter said, "or we'll have men going on leave every time we turn around."

Hope soared in Mary's chest. He was going to do something. "Papa, these are good people. I've spent time with them. They want to work."

"Yes, Mary. Let us work out the details, but I agree. For now, the injured men will keep their homes and collect their full paycheck."

Tears flowed down her cheeks. "Thank you, Papa. You are a good man."

"Now you go on to bed. We'll be here another day, so I can visit these men tomorrow."

∽

Scooter hurried down the dusty road to the hotel.

Mary was leaving in the morning, and he needed to see her one last time. To apologize.

Would she wait for him until he was older? Maybe things would be different in a few years.

If he survived working in the mine.

He circled to the side of the building. It was late, but she'd told him she was in the room facing the stable. That was how she'd sneaked out the night of the accident. He counted two windows on that side and hoped he had the right room.

Scooter picked up a rock and tossed it at the glass. In a panic, he threw two more stones without thinking. Then he saw her on the other side of the glass pane.

Mary.

He rushed forward as she pushed it open. The bottom of the window was chest high on him, so he was looking up into her sweet face.

"Scooter! If my papa catches you here, he'll have a conniption."

"I know. I had to see you."

She frowned. "Why? You said you didn't want to be friends."

Scooter flinched, then nodded. "Mary, I came to ask your forgiveness."

"You did?"

"What I said wasn't true. I want to be your friend. I—"

"Why did you say it then?"

"Your pa."

"What about him?"

"He said if I toyed with your affections, then he'd kicked my family out of the company house. Mary, I can't let that happen to my folks and my brothers and sisters. Do you understand?"

"That's terrible." Tears rolled down Mary's cheeks.

Scooter bounced on his toes and jumped, pulling himself up to straddle the window ledge. He reached for her, and she melted against him. "I love you. That's what I want to say."

She turned her face up, and he pressed his lips to

hers. Mary whimpered and wound her arms around his neck.

"We have to wait a few years," he said a few moments later, "but I won't forget you, Mary. I'll come for you as soon as I'm able, and we can be together."

She pulled back, fire in her pretty blue eyes. "It's not fair for Papa to threaten you like that. I'm fifteen years old and old enough to make my own choices."

He smoothed her hair with one hand. "He's your pa."

"I know. Oh, there's news! Papa is going to let the injured men keep their houses and full pay until they are better, or at least until February. He said it was the right thing to do and he'll tell them all tomorrow."

"You don't say." Scooter's mind raced. If his pa got a check and they stayed in the house, he'd be free to return to Pinevale Valley with Mrs. Kisselton and learn about the healing herbs. "I've got to talk to Mrs. Kisselton."

"Why? Is something wrong?"

"No." He gripped her chin and kissed her gently before jumping back to the ground. "I love you, Mary Malden."

"I love you too. And I'll wait for you. We'll be eighteen in three years," Mary said breathlessly.

"Even better, if I don't have to go into the mines, Mrs. Kisselton said I can move to Pinevale Valley and learn from her."

CHAPTER NINE

Scooter was on edge all morning, waiting for Mr. Malden to arrive at their house. He hoped Mary had been right and that her papa was really going to take care of the injured men.

"What has you all in a twist?" his ma asked.

"I can't say yet. Soon."

Mrs. Kisselton gave him a knowing look. He'd waited till she'd gotten up in the night to check on Pa and whispered his request over a cup of tea at the kitchen table. When he'd offered to work for her for room and board for a year in exchange for a chance to learn some of her knowledge, she'd readily agreed.

He hadn't told his folks yet, because he had to be certain Mr. Malden would do what Mary had said.

Ma clicked her tongue. "That driver is an hour later than he said for Mrs. Kisselton to be ready. It's almost eight o'clock."

"I—wait, is that the car?" Scooter heard the Packard 8 revving up the dirt drive. "I'll go meet him, get Pa ready," he said, racing for the porch.

Luke Mulwatter stepped out of the Packard's front seat, and Mr. Malden and his daughter Mary emerged from the back.

"Good morning, Scooter," said Mr. Malden. "I've come to speak with your pa."

"This way, sir." Scooter flourished a hand toward the door, but his eyes were glued to Mary. Her face was pink with the cold, but her smile was sweet enough to make his knees tremble.

"Scooter," she murmured.

"Come inside, Mary," Mr. Malden ordered.

She brushed past him, sliding her hand over his as she passed. It took all his control not to pull her into his arms and steal a kiss.

As he followed them inside, Mr. Malden had Mary's elbow, steering her toward Pa's bed, Mr. Mulwatter on the other side.

Ma had stuffed a blanket behind Pa to sit him up and was standing at the foot of the bed with Mrs. Kisselton.

Pa started talking as soon as they were close. "Mr. Malden. Scooter is due to come to the mine first of the week and take my place, at least until I'm able—"

Malden held up a hand. "That's why I'm here. Malden Mines is going to take care of our employees. We've decided no one is at fault in this accident, and we will continue to pay all eight of you until you can return to work."

Luke Mulwatter pushed forward with a scowl. "Not indefinitely. We'll give you until February first on the outside. If you can't work by then, the pay will be cut off, and either Scooter goes into the mine or you lose the house. We'll also be checking in on your progress."

"That's very generous of you."

"You can thank my daughter. She convinced me it was the right thing to do, and I agreed with her. The mine will survive a few months short one digging team. After all, we are down a tunnel. Tunnel three will be sealed off permanently, and no more digging will be done on the east side of the mine, in case that tar substance surfaces again."

"I'm glad to hear it," Ma said.

Mr. Malden turned to Mrs. Kisselton. "I apologize for my delay in coming here this morning."

"When will we leave for Pinevale?"

"Not till tomorrow, I'm afraid. I need to meet with the other families, and it will be too late to drive in one day."

∽

Mary tapped her foot. "Papa. Don't forget your promise."

He pressed a kiss to her forehead. "My darling daughter, I'll never forget anything with you around." Then he addressed Scooter and Mrs. Kisselton.

"Mrs. Kisselton. You helped these men and asked nothing in return. I have learned much in the past few days and realized some things I don't find appealing about myself.

She chuckled. "Mr. Malden, we all have things about ourselves that we don't prefer."

"I'd like to thank you for using your time and resources. How much money do you want?" he asked.

She shrugged. "I don't want your money."

"You want nothing?"

"I didn't say that." She chuckled again. "If you are truly feeling generous, there is something I would ask of you."

"You saved my reputation and the good name of my mining company when you healed those men. Name what you want."

"Pinevale Valley has a growing population, and I would like to move."

"Move away?"

"No. There's land near the town square I have my eye on. I dream of building a large house there, with room for visitors."

"You want to build an inn?" Malden asked.

"Kisselton Inn has a nice ring to it."

Mr. Malden stuck out his hand for her to shake. "Done. I'll deed you an acre of land free and clear, and I'll even cosign on the banknote for you to get the loan."

"That would be wonderful." Mrs. Kisselton smiled.

Mary held her breath, hoping her papa would also mend his fences with Scooter, the boy she loved and planned to love forever.

"Scooter," Papa said.

"Yes, sir?"

"I'm sorry about ... the promise I extracted from you. My daughter is her own person and fancies being in love with you for reasons I cannot fathom."

"Papa."

He snorted and gathered her against his side. "Scooter, your family is safe in their home; if you choose to correspond with my daughter from Bakersbee, that will be fine."

"Thank you, Papa." Mary flung her arms around him.

Scooter grinned. "Thank you, sir. As soon as my pa is up and around, I'm moving to Pinevale Valley to study herbs with Mrs. Kisselton. If I can save enough money, I want to attend medical school."

"You don't say." Mr. Malden's eyebrows climbed up on his forehead.

"And sir? I love your daughter with my whole heart."

CHAPTER TEN

Four years later.

Bakersbee, GA 1932

Scooter took a deep breath. The scent of home, cut lumber, mining dust, and winter wind filled his lungs. It was good to be home. If only for a visit. He still had one more year of medical school at Duke University and would bring his family back to Bakersbee.

"Are you alright?" Mary asked.

Chuckling, he put his hands on her hips, but thought

better of spinning her around and tucked her into his side instead.

It was her turn to laugh. "Spin me around right now, and this baby might appear before we're ready."

"I want to be safe in Pinevale Valley before my son—"

"Or daughter—"

"Makes an appearance." He guided her to the steps of the general store. "Have I mentioned how much I love you, Mrs. Wagner?"

"Only once or twice today." She grinned, but then her smile faded, and she indicated a little girl slumped on the steps.

"I'll check on her," Scooter said, jogging over to check on the child. He crouched down to her level. "Hello. My name's Scooter. What's your name?"

"I'm Becky," the girl said with a sniffle.

"Is something wrong, Becky?"

"I fell and hurt my wrist."

"Can I see?" Scooter held a hand palm out and waited to see if the girl would trust him.

He aimed to help others with the skills he had learned and was still learning. Someday, he'd return to Bakersbee and serve the people of this community. Being a doctor was a dream he was fulfilling, but his true purpose in life was to love his beautiful wife. She filled his heart in every way.

ABOUT PINEVALE VALLEY

The First Coast Romance Writers are happy to present the Shared World Series of Pinevale Valley. This is a multi-genre small-town romance series.

Each book will be available for at least one year from publication. Don't miss your chance to purchase this romance novel while it's available.

Check out the Pinevale Valley series:

Proceeds benefit First Coast Romance Writers, an independent non-profit organization that helps writers hone their craft and expand their knowledge of the publishing industry.

For other FCRW titles, check our our anthologies: https://firstcoastromancewriters.com/anthologies/

OTHER BOOKS BY SARA J. WALKER

Romancing the Holidays, Volume 1: The Luckiest Hat: Enjoy this heartwarming tale of two souls who meet in the most unlikely way on a windy beach in Georgia.

Romancing the Holidays, Volume 2: Miracle de Noël: Just home from the great war, a wounded man and his young wife struggle to understand the past and rebuild their future. All seems lost until an unexpected miracle brings the family back together.

Romancing the Holidays, Volume 3: Frankie's Girl She's infatuated with another, but he knows she's the one for him. Can he win her heart?

Romancing the Tropics, Volume 1: The Past and the Present Collide in Paradise 1979. A couple gets their second chance at happiness in the ash of a volcano on the Isle of Barbados.

Romancing the Tropics, Volume 2: The Gardener's Secret. In the tranquil beauty of the Keys, love and deception collide. Will their journey lead to healing or heartbreak?

For the Love of Winter: A Collection of Holiday Romances: His Christmas Date. Will the spirit of Christmas help Dino Dudley and Hilde McQuire bridge the gap between the past and a shared future?

The Grumpy Guardian's Redemption by Sara J. Walker: A heartwarming Christian story of redemption, healing, and the transformative power of love that will leave you feeling uplifted and inspired.

For the Love of Winter Volume two: A Collection of Holiday Romances: Happily Ever After, Take Two. Will Dino and Hilde's second chance at love overcome family doubts and past mistakes for a lifetime of happiness?

Coming Soon:

December 2024, The sequel to *The Grumpy Guardian's Redemption*.

ABOUT SARA J. WALKER

Sara J. Walker delights in exploring various literary genres, but her true passion is crafting heartwarming Christian romance stories. She is known for her captivating historical and contemporary stories, with quirky characters searching for their happily ever after. She balances her creative endeavors with the busy charm of small-town life and when not at her keyboard, she cherishes time with her family.

For the latest updates on Sara's works in progress and upcoming releases, visit her website at sarajwalker.com and subscribe to her newsletter.